The 3 Trees

Adapted by Gabriel Ringlet
Illustrated by Daniella Oh

Pauline
BOOKS & MEDIA
Boston

Once, on a high mountaintop, there were three beautiful little trees,
and each of them had a wonderful dream.

3

The first tree
loved to look up at the stars in the night sky.
"They shine so brightly," it thought.
"They are just like diamonds!
When I grow up,
I want to hold something special that sparkles
like a star.

"I wish to be the most beautiful treasure chest
in the world!"

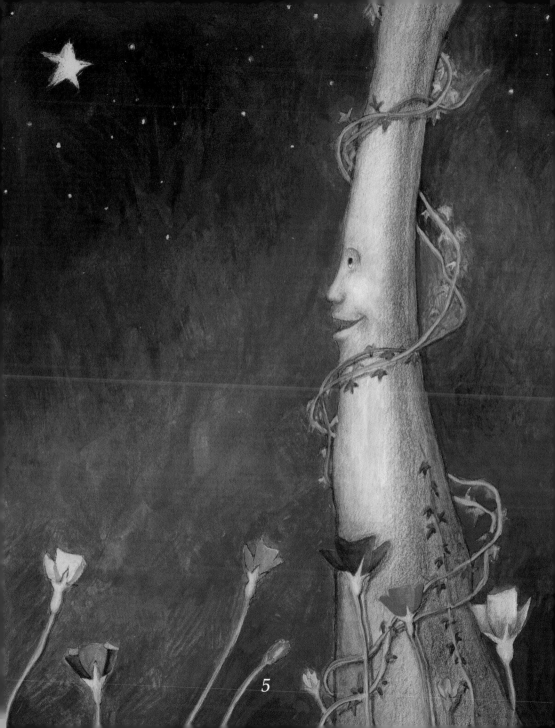

The second tree loved to look
at the little stream far below
that sparkled at night just like the stars.
But this tree was dreaming about the ocean.
"One day," it said,
"I want to sail on the mighty ocean
and carry powerful kings.

"I want to be the strongest sailing ship
in the world!"

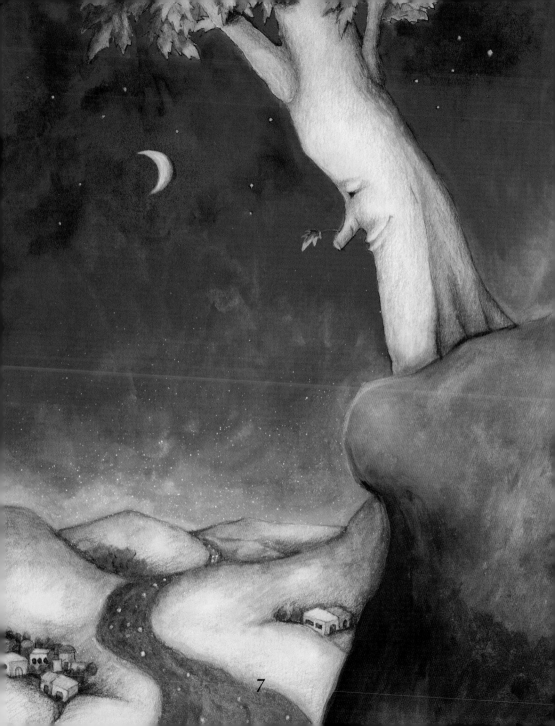

The third little tree
looked down at the stream and up at the stars.
It thought for a while and said,
"I don't want to leave this mountaintop.
I want to grow so tall
that when people lift their eyes up
to look at me,
they will think of God.

"I wish to be the tallest tree in the world
and be closest to God."

The years passed,
spring came and went many times,
and all three of the trees grew tall.

One day
three woodcutters
climbed up the mountain.

The first woodcutter
saw the first tree and said,

"Just look at this beautiful tree
It's exactly what I need."
And with one blow, he choppe
the tree down.

"At last!" said the first tree.
"I will soon be able to hold
a great treasure!"

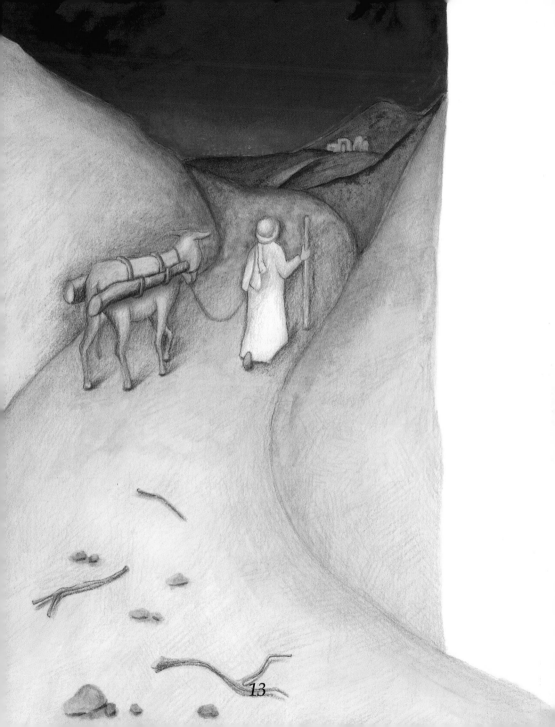

The second woodcutter
saw the second tree and said,

"Look how strong this tree is!
It's just what I need."
And with one blow, he chopped it down.

"Thank goodness! About time,"
said the second tree.
"I will soon be able to carry
powerful kings across the ocean."

14

The third woodcutter
saw the third tree and said,

"Look how straight this tree is!
It's just what I need."
And with one blow, he chopped it down.

"There goes my dream!"
thought the third tree,
and it began to sulk.

The first tree
was filled with joy
when the woodcutter
carried it
to the carpenter's shop.
Was it going to become
a treasure chest?
No, the woodcutter
made it into a manger
for the animals.

The second tree
couldn't stop smiling
when the woodcutter took it
to the shipyard.
Now for the mighty ocean!
But the workmen made it
into a small fishing boat
only big enough to carry
the day's catch from the lake.

18

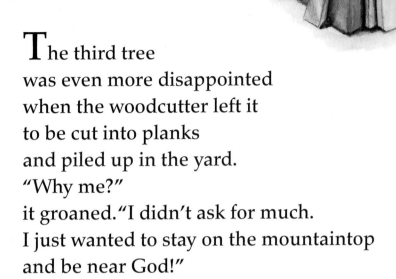

The third tree
was even more disappointed
when the woodcutter left it
to be cut into planks
and piled up in the yard.
"Why me?"
it groaned. "I didn't ask for much.
I just wanted to stay on the mountaintop
and be near God!"

Many days and nights passed,
and the dreams
of the three little trees faded
with the seasons.

Then one night
the first tree was woken up
by a young mother putting her newborn baby
into the manger.
"I wish I'd been able to get you a cradle,"
said the man with her.
"Don't worry," said the mother.
"Look how beautiful this manger is!"

And it was true. The manger sparkled
just like a star.
The first tree knew
it was holding
the greatest treasure in the world.

21

One night many years later, a strange passenger was lying fast asleep in an old fishing boat when a violent storm broke overhead.

The second little tree had seen plenty of storms,
but it thought this one would surely be its last!
The passenger woke up,
stood, and stretched his arms out to the sea,
and the storm stopped at once.
Then the second little tree knew
it was carrying
the greatest King in the world.

Some time later, on a Friday,
the third tree was still miserable
but got a surprise when someone took
an interest in its planks
piled up against the wall.

How dreadful it was, though,
to be carried across town
with everyone shouting insults
and, even worse, to feel
the hands and feet of a man
being nailed onto you!

For two days the third tree couldn't sleep.
But at dawn on Sunday morning,
new leaves suddenly started to grow
from its arms. It was amazing!

And at that moment this little tree knew
it was taller than it had dreamed possible,
for no one in the world had ever been
as close to God as it had been!

Library of Congress Cataloging-in-Publication Data

Ringlet, Gabriel.
  [3 arbres. English]
  The 3 trees / adapted by Gabriel Ringlet ; illustrated by Daniella Oh ;
[translation by Wendy Brennan].-- 1st North American ed.
     p. cm.
  Summary: Three trees that dream of greatness are surprised by the way
their dreams come true.
  ISBN 0-8198-7426-4
  [1. Folklore--Lebanon. 2. Jesus Christ--Folklore. 3. Trees--Folklore.] I. Title:
Three trees. II. Oh, Daniella, ill. III. Brennan, Wendy. IV. Title.
  PZ8.1.R4493Aah 2008
  398.2--dc22

                                                      2008001448

Original title, *Les 3 Arbres* © 2005, Éditions Médiaspaul, France
English language edition first published in 2007 by St. Pauls Publications,
    Strathfield, Australia
Translation by Wendy Brennan © St. Pauls Publications, Australia

First North American edition, 2008

Published by Pauline Books & Media, 50 Saint Pauls Avenue, Boston, MA 02130-3491

Printed in Korea

T3TS SIPSKOGUNKYO8-1010 7426-4

Pauline Books & Media is the publishing house of the Daughters of St. Paul, an international
congregation of women religious serving the Church with the communications media.

For the location of the Pauline Books & Media centers closest to you,
visit www.pauline.org.

2 3 4 5 6 7 8 9   15 14 13 12 11